Tip Tap Pans

Written by Catherine Baker
Photographed by Will Amlot

Collins

Sit in a pit.

Dan

pit

pan

mat

3

Dip in a tin.

Nan

tin

pit

pan

5

Dan tips a tin.

Tip tap tip tap.

7

Dan pats a pan.

Pit pat pit pat.

Nan taps a pan.

Tap tip tap tip.

Nan pats a tin.

Pat pit, pat pit.

After reading

Letters and Sounds: Phase 2

Word count: 48

Focus phonemes: /s/ /a/ /t/ /p/ /i/ /n/ /m/ /d/

Common exception word: a

Curriculum links: Expressive arts and design: Exploring and using media and materials ... make music

Early learning goals: Reading: use phonic knowledge to decode regular words and read them aloud accurately, read some common irregular words

Developing fluency

- Your child may enjoy hearing you read the book.
- Read page 10 and ask your child to read the sound words on page 11 (*tap tip tap tip*), doing actions as they read.
- Now do the same with pages 12 to 13.

Phonic practice

- Turn to page 11. Say the word **tap**. Ask your child if they can sound out each of the letter sounds in the word **tap** (t/a/p) and then blend them. Now ask them to do the same with the word **tip**.
- Can they read **tap, tip, tap, tip**, emphasising the /p/ sound (with a short "p", rather than a long "puh")?

Extending vocabulary

- Look at the picture on pages 6 and 7 and read the text to your child: **Dan tips a tin.**
- Ask your child if they can think of any other words we could use to describe what Dan is doing, instead of **tips**. (e.g. *shakes*, *rattles*)
- Now do the same with pages 8 and 10.
- Look at the "I spy sounds" pages (14–15) together. How many words can your child point out that contain the /t/ sound? (e.g. *tambourine*, *teddy*, *truck*, *trike*, *turtle*, *tissue*, *torch*, *twigs*, *tablecloth*)